LIONEL·AND·LOUISE

LIONEL ·AND· ·LOUISE·

by Stephen Krensky
pictures by Susanna Natti

Dial Books for Young Readers
NEW YORK

For my sister
S. K.

To Emily J.
S.N.

Published by Dial Books for Young Readers
A Division of Penguin Books USA Inc.
375 Hudson Street
New York, New York 10014

Printed in Hong Kong by South China Printing Company (1988) Limited
The Dial Easy-to-Read logo is a registered trademark of
Dial Books for Young Readers, a division of
Penguin Books USA Inc., ®TM 1,162,718.
First Edition
1 3 5 7 9 10 8 6 4 2
Library of Congress Cataloging in Publication Data
Krensky, Stephen.
Lionel and Louise / by Stephen Krensky ; pictures by Susanna Natti.
p.   cm.
Summary: Four stories about Lionel and his big sister
Louise at the beach, cleaning up a mess, fighting a "dragon,"
and camping out in the backyard.
ISBN 0-8037-1055-0 (trade). — ISBN 0-8037-1056-9 (lib. bdg.)
[1. Brothers and sisters — Fiction.] I. Natti, Susanna, ill.
II. Title.
PZ7.K883Lio 1992 [E] — dc20 91-16992 CIP AC
The full-color artwork was prepared using pencil,
colored pencils, and watercolor washes.
It was then color-separated and reproduced as
red, blue, yellow, and black halftones.

Reading Level 2.0

CONTENTS

THE RESCUE

Lionel's big sister Louise
was reading a book on her bed.
Suddenly the door burst open.
Lionel came in.
He was wearing his sword.
"I have come to rescue you
from the castle tower,"
said Sir Lionel.

"Not now," said Louise.

"I'm just getting to the good part."

"I know a giant is holding

you prisoner," said Sir Lionel.

"He's big and strong

and eats bones for breakfast."

Louise buried her head in her book.

"Go away," she said.

Sir Lionel looked around.

"Or maybe a witch has you

under a spell," he said.

"She has a lumpy nose

and snakes in her hair."

Louise shook her head.

"No witch is bothering me,"
she said.

"Only you are bothering me."

Sir Lionel stared at the window.

A fly was buzzing against the glass.

"Look out!" he cried.

"There is a dragon behind you.

It has great wings and sharp claws."

Louise rolled her eyes.

"Do you mind?" she said.

"I am trying to read."

"How can you read?" said Sir Lionel.

"The dragon may burn you to a crisp."

He took out his sword.

"Do you want to fight, dragon?"

he asked.

Louise put down her book.

She got off her bed

and opened the window.

Sir Lionel watched the dragon

fly outside.

He was pleased.

"I scared him away," he said,

putting down his sword.

"You are safe now."

Louise picked up her book.

"Does that mean you are leaving?"

she asked.

Sir Lionel did not answer her.

He was already gone.

A busy knight never stays

in one place too long.

AT THE BEACH

Lionel and Louise were at the beach
with their parents.

Louise was swimming in the ocean.

She always jumped right in.

Lionel was waiting for the water
to warm up.

He filled his pail with wet sand
and made a tower.

Then he made three more towers

and a wall to connect them.

Louise came out of the water.

"What are you making?" she asked.

"A sand castle," said Lionel.

"Do you want to help?"

"No, no," said Louise.

"I'm too grown-up for such things."

Lionel shrugged.

He started building an inner wall.

Louise watched him.

"The towers should be taller,"

she said.

"Well," said Lionel, "the waves—"

"Here," said Louise, "I'll show you."

She built up the towers.

"That's better," she said.

"Now put little ridges on top
of the walls."

"There's no time," said Lionel.

"The waves—"

"And maybe put in a village," said Louise. "Think big."

"I don't know," said Lionel.

"The waves—"

"Honestly, Lionel," said Louise. "Just watch."

Louise scooped and dug
all over the place.
When she finished, she stuck
a little stick in the tallest tower.
"That is a flag," she explained.
"The flag of Castle Louise.

It will stand forever."

A wave lapped at the base of the wall.

Some sand crumbled away.

"We are under attack!" cried Louise.

Lionel nodded.

"The tide is coming in," he said.

"We need a moat," said Louise.

She quickly dug a long ditch.

The next wave filled it in.

The water felt good

between Lionel's toes.

He stood up and stretched.

"Where are you going?" said Louise.

"In the ocean," said Lionel.

"The water is just right."

"You can't go now!" said Louise.

"What about saving my castle?"

"Good luck!" said Lionel.

And he ran off into the water.

FOOTPRINTS

Lionel was sitting in the kitchen
reading a book.
Louise came in holding a jar
of tadpoles.
She slowly climbed the stairs
and put the tadpoles in her room.
"There," she said. "Safe and sound."
When she turned around,
she saw muddy footprints
on the rug.

She followed them down the stairs
and through the hall to the kitchen.
"Lionel," she shouted, "why didn't you
tell me my sneakers were dirty?"
Lionel looked up.
"I wasn't watching," he said.
Louise sighed.

"I'll have to clean this up fast.

Father and Mother will be home soon.

They are just across the street."

She filled a pail with soap and water.

Then she got the mop and sponge.

Lionel watched her.

He knew how Louise must feel.

It was not a good feeling.

"I'll help you," he said.

"Really?" said Louise.

"Thanks. I'll do the kitchen.
You start in the hall."

Lionel scrubbed the carpet.

The footprints spread into

brown smudges.

Lionel rubbed harder.

The smudges got bigger.

Louise finished in the kitchen.

She came out to see

how Lionel was doing.

"*Arrrgh!*" she screamed.

"Well, I'm not done yet,"

said Lionel.

"I can see that," said Louise.

She took the sponge from Lionel.

Then she rubbed really hard.

She squeezed the dirty sponge

into the pail again and again.

Lionel got fresh water

from the kitchen three times.

When they finished the last footprint,

Louise let out a deep sigh.

Then she turned around.

"Oh, no!" she cried.

"Look at the wall!"

Lionel looked.

His fingerprints were everywhere.

"I'll get more water,"

he said quickly.

"No, no," said Louise.

"Don't move."

She ran for some towels

and fresh water.

Then she scrubbed and cleaned

and scrubbed some more.

Lionel held the dirty towels.

Finally she was done.

Louise slumped into a chair.

"Where should I put the towels?"
Lionel asked.

"I'll take them," said Louise.

"Why don't you go out and play?"

"Are you sure?" Lionel asked.

Louise nodded. "I'm sure.

I'm positive!

Thanks for your help, Lionel.

But, please...Go!"

"Okay," he said.

He was glad he had helped Louise.

Maybe he would try it more often.

CAMPING OUT

It was a warm summer night.

Lionel and Louise were

camping out in the backyard.

They ate a picnic dinner.

They sang songs

and looked at the stars.

Then they zipped the tent shut

and got in their sleeping bags.

Louise yawned.

"Boy, I am tired," she said.

"Me too," said Lionel.

"Good night, Lionel."

"Good night, Louise."

Lionel closed his eyes,

but he did not sleep.

The crickets were chirping too loudly.

Were they trying to warn him
about something?

Lionel poked Louise in the side.

"Are you awake?" he asked.

Louise rolled over.

"I am now," she said.

"Do you think we're safe out here?"
asked Lionel.

"Of course we're safe," said Louise.

Lionel frowned. "How can you
be so sure?" he said.

"Maybe gorillas will circle the tent
and get us."

"There are no gorillas here,"
said Louise.
"It is too far from the jungle."
"What about rhinos?"
asked Lionel.
"What if a hungry rhino
wants to eat us up?"

"A rhino could never fit in here,"
said Louise.

"The tent is too small."

Lionel had not thought of that.

He yawned.

"I guess you are right, Louise,"
he said. "Good night."

Louise grunted.

She rolled over on one side.

Then she rolled back.

But she couldn't sleep.

There were many animals

Lionel had not asked about.

There were spiders that could

tie them up in webs.

There were mice that could

nibble their toes.

And the big dog that lived next door

might come by and mistake them

for bones in the dark.

Louise sat up.

She looked at Lionel.

He was fast asleep.

She would have to stay awake

and guard them both.

Louise folded her arms and sighed.

A big sister's job was never done.